What's with this Room?

Look at this room,
it's in such distress,
you'd have to clean up
just to call it a mess.
The clutter and filth
put our house in disgrace.
What's the matter with you?
Can't you clean up this place?

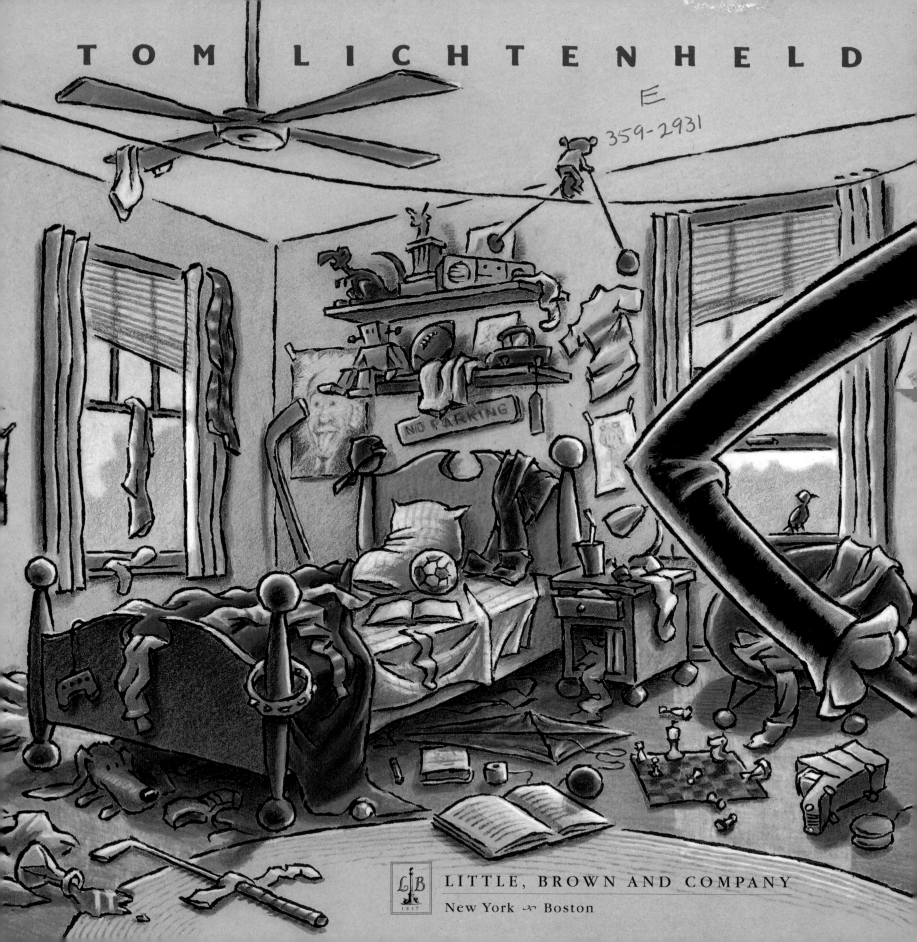

LITTLE, BROWN AND COMPANY

New York · Boston

Your stuff and your things
are in such disarray,
we just can't believe
you live here this way.
Your shoes in a pile,
your shirts in a bunch,
and there in that corner,
is that yesterday's lunch?

You take off your pants
and you just let them fall,
you throw dirty shirts
and they stick to the wall.
Your stinky old running shoes
got up and ran,
outstunk by your underwear
hung from the fan.

You used to think monsters hid under your bed,
now we think so too, but it smells like they're dead.
And even though this one looks strong as an ox,
his fatal mistake was eating your socks.

The clothing we bought
at those fancy new stores
now lies in a heap
growing fungus and spores.
While the custom-made closet
we built for these garments
has become a state refuge
for vermin and varmints.

There's lizards and lemurs
and hideous hedgehogs,
wombats and weasels
and Brazilian tree frogs.
I'm putting my foot down,
this place is a zoo.
What's this I stepped in?
It feels like gnu poo.

For your birthday we gave you

those fancy new blocks,

but you've cast them aside

and just use the box.

It houses some creature,

it's hard to tell what,

we don't want to know,

so please keep it shut.

We'd like you to tell us, your mom and your dad,
how it got in this state, how your room got this bad.
We brought you the mop, the vacuum and broom.
Now why, my dear child, won't you clean up this room?

Mom, Dad,
you don't understand.
It's not random filth,
everything's planned!
The muck and the mess
and the clothes that are cruddy,
they all play a part
in my homework and study.

I've got math, I've got science,
I've got all of those classes,
not to mention a study
of stinky shoe gases.
The crud and the critters,
they all play a part,
and if it's not science,
I just call it art.

THIS IS NOT A
PIPE, EITHER.

Those clothes aren't heaped up just because I'm a pig,
I'm actually creating an archaeological dig.
In a couple of years I'll give you a chance
to dig and discover my petrified pants.

3RD GRADE

2ND GRADE

1ST GRADE

KINDERGARTEN

That isn't just vermin down under the rugs,
I'm studying a family of misbehaved bugs.
On my knees all day Tuesday I got a bad blister
while watching a cockroach torment his young sister.

And my underwear flung on the fan is, of course,
just a method to study centrifugal force.
As they spin round and round I can measure the flows
of the air by the smells that I smell with my nose.

I'm not the first person with a closet of fur,
but mine are alive, that's what they prefer.
And while all their doo-doo is nasty to noses,
just wait 'til you see how it growses the roses.

That food in the corner,
all covered with green,
will save you big money,
come next Halloween.

With time it will turn
into sticky brown snacks
perfect for filling
those trick-or-treat sacks.

And finally here's something
of which I'm most proud
but cover your ears,
the noise could be loud.
It'll clear out your noses,
if not the whole room,
when I pour in the vinegar
and watch it go…

Although that experiment was really a blast,
it cleaned out my room just a little too fast,
Now all my pet projects have turned to debris
and taught me a lesson from up in a tree.

I'm done with excuses, it's time to confess,
that room was a pigsty, a big moldy mess.
As soon as I locate the mop and the broom,
I'll make an experiment of cleaning my room!

Copyright © 2005 by Tom Lichtenheld

Little, Brown and Company

Time Warner Book Group
1271 Avenue of the Americas, New York, NY 10020
Visit our Web site at www.lb-kids.com

First Edition:September 2005

Library of Congress Cataloging-in-Publication Data

Lichtenheld, Tom.
 What's with this room? / Tom Lichtenheld.—1st ed.
   p. cm.
  Summary: A discussion between a boy and his parents about a
bedroom, that is so dirty he would "have to clean up just to call
it a mess," ends with a blast.
 ISBN 0-316-59286-2
 [1. Cleanliness—Fiction. 2. Parent and child—Fiction. 3.
Humorous stories. 4. Stories in rhyme.] I. Title. II. Title:
What is with this room? PZ8.3.L596Wh 2005
[E]—dc22

                                      2004022709

10 9 8 7 6 5 4 3 2 1
TWP
Printed in Singapore

The illustrations for this book were done in ink, watercolor,
colored pencil, pastels, and toe jam.
The text was set in Fritz, and the display type is hand-lettered.
No gnus were harmed in the making of this book.

Book design by Tom Lichtenheld

OTHER BOOKS BY TOM LICHTENHELD

WHAT ARE YOU SO GRUMPY ABOUT?
Named one of the best children's books of 2003 by *Child* magazine
A *Kirkus Reviews* ★ Starred Review

EVERYTHING I KNOW ABOUT PIRATES
Featured in *Newsweek*'s "Books of Wonder," December 2000

EVERYTHING I KNOW ABOUT MONSTERS
"Sure to be a hit with kids" —*School Library Journal*

EVERYTHING I KNOW ABOUT CARS
A Junior Library Guild selection

Thanks to Adam Lichtenheld, whose poem "The Room of Doom" inspired this book.

To Jan, FOR HER WISDOM, IMAGINATION, AND LOVE